ABC Zoo

Rod Campbell

MACMILLAN CHILDREN'S BOOKS

a is for animals

b is for bear

c is for camel

d is for dolphin

e is for elephant

f is for fish

g is for gorilla

h is for hippo

i is for iguana

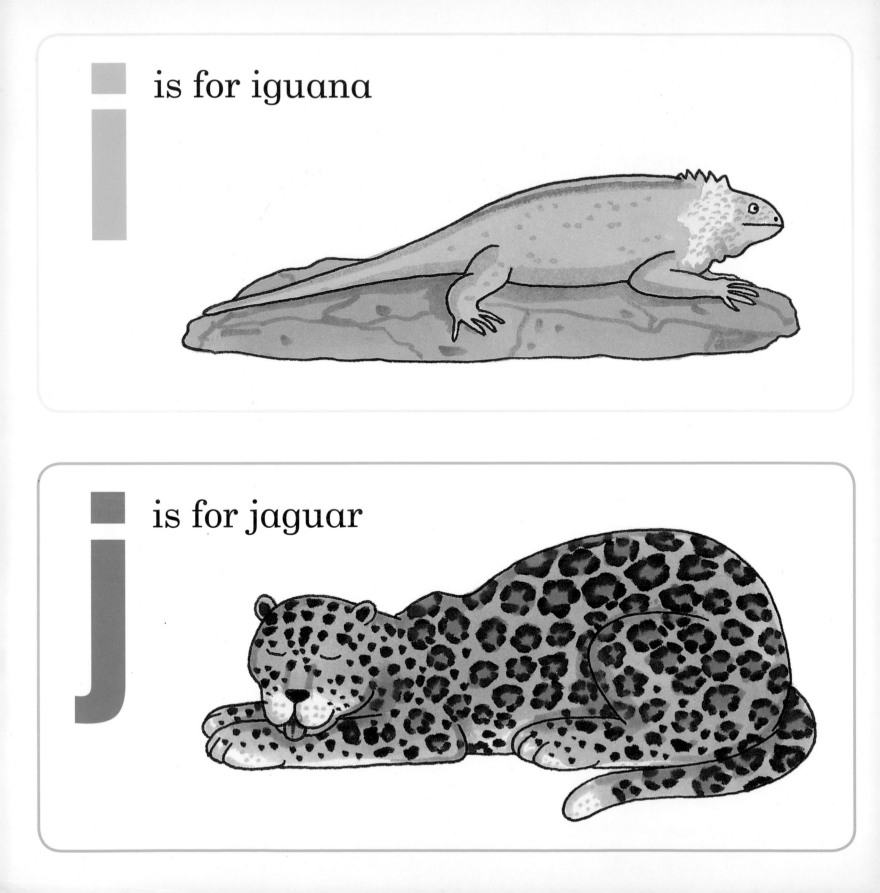

j is for jaguar

k is for koala

l is for lion

m is for monkey

n is for newt

o is for ostrich

p is for panda

q is for quail

is for raccoon

s is for snake

t is for tiger

is for
umbrella
bird

V is for
vulture

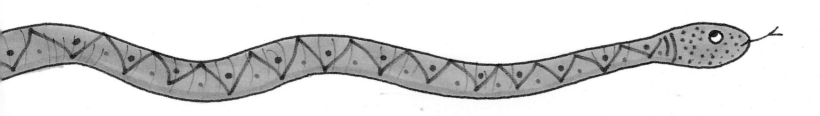

W is for walrus

X is for x-ray fish

y is for yak

z is for zebra

and also for . . .